The Murderous Mr. A

Peter J. Michael

The Murderous Mr. A

ISBN-13: 978-0-6459234-8-3

Published by Peter J. Michael

SUMMARY

Professional New York City police officers were investigating notorious organised crime killers invading the land and bidding for absolute power across all corners of the State.

Master Detective Robert Stewart was reinstated in the NYPD as Commander – and his police partner John McCallum, following his one-year absence from his official law-enforcement local police force duties, due to personal reasons dealing with family issues, was also reinstated in the New York City Police Department in one of his former ranks as Captain.

The Murderous
Mr. A

THE MURDEROUS MR. A

Fifty-eight-year-old, ruthless-looking, stocky-built Aldo Anselmo disembarked into New York City on the 1st of January 1997, bringing in the New Year's festivities in a new country in the nick of time.

He was originally from Rome, Italy where he sought to expand his criminal kingdom in the United States, primarily New York. He wanted to become the most powerful gangster in the State. And he vowed to kill, destroy and absolutely punish quite severely anyone stupid and idiotic enough who got in his way.

Aldo Anselmo was a ruthless brute of a man, with no conscious, no compassion and absolutely no mercy for his fellow human being. 'All those people are under my feet!' He would curse to his only son, thirty-one-year-old Arturo.

Arturo was a lean, yet strong-looking young man, unlike his bulky father. But similar to his evil father, he had a dark complexion and jet-black hair. But Arturo had a scalp filled with straight hair, his father had a full head of thick wavy hair.

His son had surprisingly meek features whilst his father just looked evil, intimidating and brutal with his baggy eyes and ashen-faced rugged features.

Already the Anselmo family purchased a large mansion in Brooklyn and settled into their new home quite rapidly. All the furniture arrangements and purchase of their new home was arranged days earlier, whilst they still resided in Rome.

The reason for the move to the United States quite hastily was for personal reasons, mostly relating to the son, Arturo.

Whilst in Italy, Arturo fell in love with an American woman who was holidaying alone in Rome. She lived in New York. And Arturo met her a few times at a local Italian cafeteria. He bought her coffee and breakfast on many occasions. And he thought to himself: I will have this woman. I like everything about her. Her eyes, her face, her fair skin, the plumpness of her big great breasts which bulged out of the jumper she wore in the cold weather. I know she has great legs and the best arse! She will be mine!

But the relationship in Italy was merely one of friendship. Arturo wanted more, but he knew she did not desire him as much as he desired her, sexually.

So, after two weeks, she left Rome to return to New York to reunite with her ex-boyfriend. Arturo was angry as he thought to himself evilly: You bitch! You stupid bitch! You fucking bitch! You take my free meals and then you leave me for another cock in America. No, woman! That will not happen. Either you love me or you will love no one! I will not allow you to be with anyone, but me!

So, Arturo explained the story of his falling in love with an American woman in her mid-twenties named Bice to his father Aldo. And Arturo said that he wanted to leave Rome to be with her in New York.

Aldo seemed not the least resistant in the idea. But he was really quite supportive of it. It was as if he planned to move his powerbase to the United States for some time. And now, his son gave him the perfect reason for the relocation. Perfect! Aldo smiled as he smoked an Italian cigarette and his son Arturo joined him in lighting up a thinly-brown cigar.

So, it was agreed. They would all move immediately to the United States. And in the process, Arturo could have his American woman as his wife, whilst his father looked to possess the entire city of New York at whatever cost, in order to become the most powerful gangster Crime Lord of the State and the entire United States country!

But his son Arturo did not mean to be the bearer of bad news to his father as he first insisted, they move to the United States, but still, he was not convinced that Bice would become his wife.

"Why is that?" his demented father asked in Italian, though he and his son were also quite fluent in speaking English.

Arturo replied to his father also in Italian dialect, "That bitch. Father, that bitch says she is in love with someone else in New York!"

His father said rather bluntly now in English, as if practising the native language for once they entered the United States, "It is very important to me that my son marries a woman he loves, so you can have children and continue my legacy into the next generation! NOW, if she doesn't reciprocate the same love, I can understand why you would label this woman a bitch. But my son, do not worry about it. We will make the move to the United States for the purposes of expanding my empire and forming a union with the woman of your desire. And if she refuses to wed you, I will have her mother and her father killed and I will kill that other love interest of hers. So don't worry. She will be with you by force. I will dictate her sex life on my terms – and that means, with you, my son. No one else. If she refuses to leave her other boyfriend, then I will simply eliminate him and her entire family, all her relatives, until she complies with our demands and sleeps with you and only you, my son. And if you choose, you will marry her and she will obey!"

So, the Anselmo family moved to the United States by the 1st of January 1997 and they tracked Bice, and forced her with wild threats to leave her other boyfriend and move in to the Anselmo Family Brooklyn Mansion with Arturo. She was pressured and forced to obey such strict orders.

Of course, Arturo would never trust her. So, he kept her under constant surveillance, even as she worked as a full-time nurse at the local public Brooklyn hospital. He would stalk her every move: who she visited, the phone calls she made, even imagine her every thought and aspiration. And if he even remotely suspected that she would chase the pants of that arsehole ex-boyfriend of hers, he would kidnap that prick and cut off his penis with a razorblade. She knew the ground rules. So, she would obey, or else…!

Upon threatening the lives of her ex-boyfriend and her mother and father's lives, also residing in Brooklyn, she trembled in fear and would obey the strict instructions of specifically Mob Boss Aldo Anselmo.

But she was a woman in lust for another partner. Aldo knew the character of such a woman. He had his detectives follow her surreptitiously everywhere she went. And they saw her at work during her lunch break sitting alone inside the hospital cafeteria, crying tears into a photograph of her ex-boyfriend she held in her hands, pressed to her cheek.

Aldo became angry. He instructed his son immediately what must be done in secret as he was posted inside his private study of his New York mansion with Arturo.

"That bitch hoe-bag slut wants to put another man's dick in her mouth instead of loving my son and having his children. My threat against her obviously fell on deaf ears."

That evening at midnight, Aldo Anselmo ordered two hitmen to enter the Brooklyn home of that girl Bice's parents – and kill them.

The two hitmen each carried a huge army knife as they entered the parents' house, picking the locks of the front door at night when everyone was asleep, no one witnessing anything.

Outside and inside the house was dark black, everyone asleep, including the neighbours all across the street. And the hitmen wearing balaclavas and gloves entered the parents' room. The mother and the father were snoring. They had no idea what was to happen to them and they never would, because they would not be allowed to ever wake up again. The two hitmen each placed one hand separately on their mouths as they forced them to lie on their stomachs, face-down on their bed - and with their knife-hand, stabbed the large blade into their spine, which not only would cripple them, but the knife would enter their lungs, piercing vital organs, causing them to die quite rapidly in a pool of blood! And died, they both had.

When the religious Catholic parents did not show up for Mass as per usual at the local Brooklyn Church on Sunday morning two days later, the police were called in to investigate.

Commander Robert Stewart and his police partner, Captain John McCallum were the first officers at the scene who investigated the double homicide inside the two victims' home, on 8th Avenue in Brooklyn.

Robert called police headquarters immediately upon determining the double murders of the two corpses found inside their bedroom - and had forensic investigators combing the entire house straightaway for DNA evidence: fingerprints, hair follicles, footprint evidence, the works, in order to assist in solving the two crimes; whilst he and John began questioning potential witnesses within the vicinity. They went door-to-door questioning every neighbour on the street to see if anyone saw anything. But no one had. Everyone questioned appeared shocked by the brutal murders.

Robert did a background check on the dead middle-aged couple and found they had one daughter named Bice, who was last spotted moving into the home of the notorious Anselmo family in the borough.

Robert knew about the Anselmo family criminal ties. He was investigating Mafia activities in the city and the Patriarch Aldo was now the new resident criminal in New York from Rome.

Forensic investigators were searching for clues to the identity of the killer mostly inside the home of the two deceased victims (being the official crime scene of the double murders), at the same time Robert launched his investigation into the Anselmo family's involvement in the crimes.

It was just too coincidental that the clean (no history of trouble with the law) nurse daughter of a clean (no history of trouble with the law) family of furniture retail proprietors, suddenly lived in the Anselmo mansion, then her parents wound up murdered. Robert could not help but note the serious connection here and immediately suspected Aldo Anselmo behind the murders of Bice's parents.

When Robert and his police partner John stormed the gates of the Anselmo mansion to question both the Patriarch Aldo and his only son Arturo of the crimes, they noticed that Bice was nowhere to be found.

Initially, Robert told the gate guard outside to open the gates to let them in. And then the bodyguard at the front door of the mansion was forced to let the police inside their house and invade their privacy, upon their orders to storm the fortress, so to speak.

Robert questioned both Aldo and his son Arturo who stood inside the living room looking serious-faced and awfully guilty.

"Where is the girl Bice? She was last spotted moving in here. She lived here recently! I want you to tell me where she is?" Robert demanded to know.

The criminal family's son remained mute. He appeared rather nervous and feared saying the wrong thing to the police out of that sheer fear he suddenly experienced, so he allowed his tough and brutal father Aldo do all the talking.

And Aldo was a master criminal and a master manipulator, mixed with being a master at controlling his emotions no matter what, pressure or otherwise. And he responded unemotionally by saying, "She was worried about becoming homeless for a while. She complained she had no money. So, we met her whilst living in Rome and told her that we were coming to New York to move abroad and relocate here. So, she was allowed to live with us until she landed on her feet financially. She was a proud woman, Commander. She would not accept our hospitality for long. So, she left earlier this morning at 7:00 a.m. It is now 2:40 p.m. So, she has been gone for hours now. We don't know where."

Robert's intuition was working overtime. He immediately suspected something foul in this. He knew Aldo Anselmo was lying out of his teeth.

"Did you know that her parents were murdered recently inside their home?" Robert asked rather serious-faced, holding back his anger for now at the suspected culprit villain behind their deaths.

Aldo Anselmo maintained the cool façade and replied, "No, Commander Stewart. That is a big shock to me, to us! I had no idea her parents were even living in the same city as her. Nor did I know about their misfortunate murders until you reported it to us right now!"

Robert grunted immediately, "I never told you that her parents lived here in the same city as their daughter Bice. Funny, how you seemed to have known that." Robert searched for clues with his eyes. He wanted to confirm his vivid suspicions, so he raised a curious eye at that point first, to the mute and seeming nervous son of the evil Patriarch Arturo, and then at his wicked father Aldo and back-and-forth over again and again repetitively several times, studying their eyes, their facial expressions and body gestures, until his suspicions were truly confirmed.

The son acted too quiet for his liking. He was nervous, hiding his eyes from him, pointing his eyeballs to the floor and his father seemed too cool, unemotional, and not really surprised at the reported bad news of the double homicide of the parents to the girl who was recently living here with them. Robert concluded the compunction of these two fiends as culpable in the murders just by the expression of guilt written all over their faces. They just looked like they not only knew about the murders and were not saying, but they also had a hand in the brutal deaths! In fact, they were most likely behind it all.

Robert still kept a cool impartial face as he responded to Aldo's lies and denials in knowing anything about the girl Bice's parents' deaths: "In fact, they were killed inside their own bedroom. They were sleeping inside their bed and two assailant killers snuck into their house after midnight, when everything was all dark and all the neighbours were fast asleep, seeing nothing. The killers apparently wore gloves. No fingerprints left behind, picking the locks of the front door (as no doors were jemmied and no windows broken, and nothing- no money seeming missing from their wallets found) - and the killers managed to enter their upstairs bedroom and stabbed each of them to death at the same time in the back."

Again, Robert's eyes peered back-and-forth at the two villains held in grave suspicion as primary suspects responsible for the two deaths or murders as it were. Arturo still seemed quiet as a mouse, his eyes cowering away from his police interrogator, not daring to look at him, which was suspicious enough and gave away a look of guilt to Robert instantly. And his father Aldo just shrugged his shoulders in a pretentious form of ignorant confusion and uncaring dismissal to Robert's revelations concerning the deaths.

"And now the girl Bice has disappeared!!!" Robert raised his voice to a shout in order to provoke a reaction from them this time. "WHAT DOES THAT SAY?"

And a reaction he certainly got.

The patriarch's son Arturo couldn't help but let out a nervous cough at this point and Aldo now also kept mute, but maintained his eyes coolly focused on Robert's.

Robert had enough of the lies. He knew the truth. He knew what he was going to do in order to obtain the evidence to back up his suspicions concerning the guilty behind the deaths – and also immediately, he ordered a state-wide police search party **APB** be initiated for the whereabouts of the missing twenty-five-year-old Brooklyn nurse called Bice. She was not at her usual Brooklyn flat or spotted at work all day when she was in fact rostered to be on duty at the Brooklyn hospital. Robert questioned friends and colleagues who heard nothing from her. He did a complete and thorough check of the city's bus, train, harbour and private and commercial airport terminals. Again, her name came up nowhere. She officially did not plan to leave New York again. Which led Robert to suspect foul play in her disappearance the same as the foul play determined in the deaths and confirmed homicides of her parents.

Now where Bice was concerned, Robert unfortunately suspected the worst. He believed she was dead before the active police search party officials could confirm it.

Two hours later the dead body of Bice was spotted in the Brooklyn harbour. When the police fished her body out of the river, they found she was shot in the back of the head four times, the coroner established at point-blank range. And fresh blood and skull fragments belonging to her were spotted all over the wooden decking of the pier. Which meant she was driven here first after being forced kidnapped - and then killed on the waterfront in broad daylight and following that, her dead corpse was thrown into the river.

Another homicide. Robert knew the Anselmo family was behind her death as well.

The question of **'why?'** carried many theories. Robert could only pinpoint one solid theory. Love gone wrong. A one-sided love which led to blackmail and then a triple homicide almost back-to-back!

It was not long after Robert received a call from the harbour patrol alerting him to another dead body found in the bay, floating a mile up river from where Bice's body was recently located.

The body belonged to a twenty-eight-year-old Caucasian male GP Doctor of medicine, who lived in Brooklyn but practised his business of medicine in the borough of Queens. The identity of the second corpse found today in the river was called Bart Winton. Robert did a background check on the man and found that he was also the ex-boyfriend to Bice. And after questioning Bice's friends and work colleagues, it was confirmed that Bice was interested in hooking up once more with her ex-boyfriend Bart. And now he was found dead too. And Robert's initial theory of a love gone wrong being behind Bice's death was really now confirmed by the murder of her ex-boyfriend, a boyfriend she wanted to establish close ties with again.

And when the police commander read the coroner's report into the ugly and gruesome cause of death of Bart Winton, Robert Stewart knew beyond a shadow of a doubt that the evil Anselmo family was behind it.

Bart Winton had his penis and testicles removed by a knife and the same knife was then stabbed into his heart killing him rather quickly before he was dumped into the river. When the police lab boys tore into the dead man's Brooklyn average-sized house, they found evidence of his blood, penis and testicles at the scene. So, he was killed first at his home in broad daylight. His door must have been left open. So, the killer (the coroner concluded just one), entered his home, wrestled him to the ground, pulled down his pants and removed his complete genitalia with a knife. Then used the same knife to stab him in the heart. Then wrapped his body in plastic (because no trail of blood was found leading anywhere else outside his house where the body was dragged to), and then taken obviously by motor vehicle to be dumped into the river without the plastic wrapper. The plastic wrapper was first removed on purpose as if the killer was ordered out of spite to make the body be found.

And judging by the gruesome and bloody personal nature of that maniacal crime, the motivation was certainly that of a jealous lover's murderous rampage, meaning Arturo –

and his father Aldo carried out the murder for his son on Bart, Bice and her parents. So far, the Anselmo family disembarked into New York just several days ago, and the death toll already by their grubby destructive hands was four. Robert knew he had to establish concrete evidence of the criminal activities concerning the Anselmo family - or else the four corpses found so far would seem as duck walk compared to the mass murdering death-inflicting carnival of horrors to come by this brutal and mean-spirited family!

Robert again confronted Aldo and his son Arturo Anselmo inside their 8,000 square foot in interior space high society mansion, situated on a 30-acre land on 18th Avenue in Brooklyn. Robert questioned his two primary targets now concerning the murders of Bice and Bart and also received evasive answers to his questions. Robert hinted particularly to Aldo, the patriarch of the family and suspected mastermind behind those additional two killings as well: "Don't make yourself too comfortable, because I'll be back and I'll keep coming back, until I have an arrest warrant for the murderers responsible for these four homicides who will each receive life sentences for their bloody crimes. That's not a threat, it's a guarantee!"

Robert Stewart immediately began his investigation into the illegal operations of the Anselmo family. He put all the main players under surveillance using both his local police and SIA international government agency resources and manpower, stopping at nothing until he nailed all of them to the wall.

Robert quickly uncovered evidence of one of the Anselmo family employee's corruption. The Anselmo family had vested interests in many businesses, even charity organisations. Apparently one of the employees of a Bronx private hospital funded by the Anselmo family (as Aldo sat as major stockholder); the main accountant was stealing prescription drugs from the hospital and selling it to pushers on the street, then the pushers were consecutively selling the drugs to potential addicts. That same employee was also under police surveillance when caught red-handed skimming monetary funds from the hospital. Robert arrested him immediately for embezzlement and drug dealing. That was one-man down so far in the Anselmo family and many others to go.

One week later, police uncovered that a front man crook for the Anselmo family had placed a contract out on the life of Captain John McCallum, who vowed to clean up the filthy Anselmo Mob from existence in his city. The front man crook was the police chief commissioner of the 25th division precinct station house of Brooklyn, New York, where both Robert Stewart and John McCallum operated inside.

Robert organised thorough and discreet surveillance on all members of the Anselmo family. And through extensive wiretapping, overheard the corrupt police chief commissioner of his precinct telephone captains of the Anselmo Family Empire, alerting them of Captain John McCallum's very vocal threats against the Mob in question, within the walls of his precinct, directed to all the officers beneath him. So, the Mob captains ordered a hit on the police captain.

That night as John entered his Brooklyn home after work, he found three masked gunmen waiting for him inside his living room once he turned on the lights. But the gunmen were also surprised when an army of police led by Robert Stewart were onto them, swarming the entire vicinity of the premises inside-and-outside in secret, which resulted in a bloody gun battle between the mob and the police in order to save John's life. The three gunmen were fatally cut down eventually by the police bullets.

But three police officers received multiple gunshot wounds in the line of fire saving the life of Captain John McCallum. Two of them were sent to hospital in critical condition and one of them died at the scene inside John's house from a fatal gunshot wound to the head.

The three mob captains tape-recorded ordering the hit against the life of John McCallum had warrants issued for their arrests. The police tracked them down at a local strip club in the Bronx. They foolishly resisted arrest by the police and also tried to fire back their heavy artillery at law-enforcement officials, but this time, the police got lucky and cut them down in bloody fashion; they cut them dead before the mob captain assassins could successfully injure or kill any further police officials.

Robert Stewart arrested the middle-aged corrupt mafia-bribed police chief commissioner of his precinct. Robert vowed that dirty cop on the take for the mob would receive life imprisonment for his crimes.

Aldo Anselmo soon felt the walls of his empire caving in around him. For solace and comfort, he entered the arms of his fifty-year-old Italian wife Barbara. Barbara resisted his embrace and ducked away his advances toward her. She long suspected his evil schemes and two-faced façade. But when she witnessed multiple police visits to her home now stationed in New York with her family, she knew her husband was bad, very bad, extremely bad news and she did not want him to touch her. She shoved away his embraces and turned down his invitation inside their bedroom for sex.

The next evening, Aldo Anselmo, accompanied with eight bodyguards, went to visit a friendly-faced long-time resident of New York City named Sam Cornelli, owner of one of the grandest and most famous nightclub-restaurants in Brooklyn, New York. Aldo Anselmo wanted to make an offer to Sam Cornelli for his nightclub business. He wanted to buy and takeover ownership of his nightclub-restaurant.

Sam Cornelli was immediately offended and refused Aldo Anselmo's offer to buy his thriving business and take away his livelihood from him.

But Sam Cornelli knew of Aldo Anselmo's disgusting reputation. He knew of his Mafia ties. He also knew that everyone who came in contact with this Mafia Chieftain became afraid of him. But even though Aldo Anselmo was an intimidating man, Sam stood his ground firmly with a blunt 'NO' to his offer to buy his business. He would not sell his livelihood to him. His 'NO' was final. And he would never change his mind, no matter what!

Two nights later, Aldo Anselmo's wife Barbara again refused her husband's invitation inside their bed for sex. She also gave him a firm 'NO' to his longing for her soft-skinned naked body and feminine assets.

That night she said she would sleep in one of the guest rooms in order to teach her husband a lesson for his bad ways.

She also was concerned for their son Arturo's welfare. She knew Aldo was grooming him to be evil like him, so she concocted a scheme to save her son by telling Aldo that Arturo really was NOT his son. She hinted that just as he was an adulterer, she too had an affair long ago with one of the family's chefs in Rome - and he was Arturo's father. His real father.

Aldo blew up at his wife for the first time in their over-thirty-years-of-marriage and shouted, "What the hell are you saying, you foolish woman. Are you saying that my beloved Arturo is really not the son of my seed?"

His wife cursed in tears in a desire to save her only son: "Yes. Yes. Yes!" she shouted.

Aldo was not easily fooled. "You give me solid proof of your diabolical words before I shall believe such a ridiculous claim!"

Meanwhile, Robert Stewart began his eavesdropping and snooping investigations against Aldo Anselmo's current criminal activities, as well as his retrieving all background information concerning the evil crime chief, when Robert Stewart overheard Aldo Anselmo's private phone conversations he conducted using the private phone inside his limousine, specifically his current plans, of using one of Sam Cornelli's bookkeepers (serving as a double agent for the mob), to blackmail and threaten Sam Cornelli to sell his nightclub-restaurant to Aldo Anselmo.

The American bookkeeper named Brad Mouse would rig the accounting books of the business to make it seem as though Sam was laundering large amounts of drug money into his nightclub-restaurant - and would use that as leverage to blackmail Sam Cornelli to sell his business to the mob - or else the books would be turned over to the authorities, specifically the IRS. And Sam would go to prison.

Despite the tampering of the books, Sam Cornelli ignored the mob's vehement warnings in refusing to sell his business to them.

Barbara Anselmo persisted in her tale to her husband Aldo that their son Arturo really did not carry his blood into his veins. She still continued telling her husband that he was not Arturo's biological father, so that he would let his son go away from his evil clutches and not proceed in his scheme to have their son possessed by his evil ways - at the same time as Aldo would stop pressuring her for sex, if he believed she lied to him about Arturo's real paternity all along, for decades, and was an unfaithful wife to him.

Meanwhile - Robert Stewart studied the blueprints of the Anselmo mansion in Brooklyn - and discovered a secret passage inside the Anselmo residence living room floor, which led, by a wooden stairway, to a secret tunnel underneath the house, that covered most of Brooklyn. For instance, the secret tunnel system underneath the Anselmo mansion house and acreage outside, travelled to a big part of Brooklyn, with another secret passage into the tunnel which opened inside the downstairs cellar of Sam Cornelli's nightclub-restaurant also in the borough.

Using top-secret government files, Robert tracked not only the secret tunnel system in Brooklyn, but both its entrances through secret passages inside the Anselmo mansion living room and the cellar basement area of Sam Cornelli's nightclub-restaurant.

Robert Stewart overheard the evil mob boss's persistent phone calls inside his limousine, to his mole accountant Brad Mouse, situated inside the Sam Cornelli nightclub-restaurant, forcing the bribed accountant to go against Sam, so that Aldo could take over the nightclub-restaurant business.

One week later, Aldo Anselmo threatened his wife Barbara never to tell their son that he was not his father or else he would punish her severely. He threatened to have her committed to a mental hospital if she ever breathed a word of her lies to their son. And Barbara knew her evil husband was serious in his threat to have her locked up in a nut house forever.

The next evening, Robert intercepted a meeting being hosted between Aldo Anselmo and local Mafia bigshots, secretly gathered inside his mansion.

They all entered his home with faces concealed by large hats and sunglasses even after midnight. And they attended his home separately and in normal vehicles, nothing fancy, not to arouse law-enforcement suspicion. They intended on entering his house after midnight in disguise and secretly, careful they were not being tailed.

Robert would record their conversations and foil their sick and evil plans. And it so happened, that Robert Stewart was the main topic of their discussion.

"Tell me about him, this famous cop!" Aldo Anselmo insisted to the well-dressed mob boss biggies, who gathered inside his home even with respective bodyguards assembled by their sides, much like well-mannered comrades.

The current syndicate bosses of New York City all hinted almost at the same time with eyes wide open, alert and seeming rather startled at the mentioning of this particular nuisance cop: "Yes. We have certainly heard about him. He ruined our predecessors. He caused many bigshots' downfalls. He's dangerous to us. He is not one to be toyed with. We cannot let him ever get too close to us!"

Robert knew the insinuations being concocted between the lines. But Robert planned to get them before they ever got him, specifically the most powerful of them all, Aldo Anselmo.

Barbara Anselmo in fear of her life kept quiet about her lie of her son concerning his true paternity.

And before long, Arturo did confront his father privately inside his living room saying, "My father, I feel it was a mistake to kill all those people. I mean Bice and her ex-boyfriend and her parents. I wish you did not do that!"

But Aldo Anselmo insisted, "My son, they deserved to die. I threatened that girl to be with you. She refused. So, I simply made good on my threat and as a consequence, they all died. They just had to die! I cannot allow anyone to betray my son, just as I cannot allow anyone to betray me!"

Gotcha! Robert Stewart clenched his jaw, as he and his police partner John McCallum were surreptitiously planted inside the secret dark tunnels (lit only by their personal torches in their hands), underneath the echoing wooden floorboards of the Anselmo mansion living room, as they overheard and tape-recorded every admission of murder and conspiracy for murder that was spoken. Robert now had the evidence to arrest Aldo Anselmo at any time. But he was going to build the strongest case possible. He wanted to gather all the dirt on Aldo. And he was determined to get it.

In order to keep her bad husband away from her, Barbara yet maintained the story only for her husband's ears that Arturo was not his son.

The next evening, Robert Stewart and John McCallum entered the secret passage floorboard opening of the tunnel system leading into the Anselmo house living room.
Robert first made a call to his locally-planted SIA cohorts from his cellular phone.
He arranged for his government department infiltrators to have the electricity supply to the Anselmo mansion cut off, as well as temporarily disabling the standby backup power generators, which stopped all power to the hidden surveillance cameras inside the Anselmo house, so the mob would not know of the police invading their privacy by entering their personal space of residence.

The Anselmos were busy celebrating their son's 32nd birthday at Sam Cornelli's nightclub-restaurant.

No servants or bodyguards in sight at the mansion.

So, Robert and John, with torches at hand, began searching the entire house for more evidence of the Anselmo family's illegal activities.

Robert located a safe hidden behind a wall painting inside the master bedroom.

Robert and John used their special police training skills and tools to open the safe without damaging the locks or the safe itself - and located a three-inch-thick folder of files inside there. It seemed as though Mob Boss Aldo Anselmo accumulated confidential information on all various players connected to his life in New York. He had information on everyone's life. He even had a file on Robert and John as local police heavies. He wanted to know everything about everyone and how all these different people affected him.

Robert and John took snapshots of the files and placed everything inside the safe as it was, before he and John left the scene as they entered, disappearing without a trace inside the living room secret floorboard passage, which led into the secret tunnels, which so far, even

Aldo Anselmo was unaware of its existence beneath the floors of his domain. The Anselmo mansion's power supplies were also restored following the exit of the two police investigators.

Within a twenty-four-hour space of time, Robert had a secret meeting with Sam Cornelli inside the cellar of his Brooklyn-based restaurant-nightclub.

He explained to Sam, "I am very close to nailing Aldo Anselmo to the wall. In fact, I already have the goods on him. But, in order to get more information on Aldo Anselmo, I want you to pretend that you will allow him to buy your nightclub-restaurant."

His old friend Sam Cornelli was curious as he asked, "Why?"

Robert responded, "I have reason to believe that Aldo Anselmo wants to buy this place to run drugs inside it. He wants to use it as a front for people to come in here, and purchase the drugs, as well as using an otherwise legitimate establishment as your business, to rig the books so he can launder his vast drug profits through. I am thoroughly investigating his illegal activities. I have been going all the way as far as his life in Rome. So far, I know he has hired lackeys to 'illegally' take vast sums of money out of Italy and send it here into the States. This money he has accumulated from running illegal rackets in Rome such as grand larceny, bank robbery, extortion, loan-sharking and drug dealing. And he wants to take over large businesses all across the state of New York, such as your nightclub-restaurant, to use these unassuming legitimate businesses to the outside world, as a criminal base for drug dealing - and tampering the books for money laundering the illegal drug profits inside them also, so he can escape detection. Now, I want to stop him from getting away with this. So, pretend you will sell this business of yours to him, and that will lead us to newer and additional charges against him, before he ever gets a chance to force the signature of sale of your legitimate enterprise to his family empire."

Sam Cornelli understood everything and responded with a big: OK!

Aldo Anselmo's instincts told him that his wife Barbara was lying about her claims that Arturo was not his son, so he did not even bother ordering up any tests, such as DNA testing, to prove that Arturo was his son. He knew Arturo was his flesh and blood from his birth - and would continue treating him as a son without any, in his mind, foolish need for confirmation to the truth.

Robert Stewart began his intense Organised Crime Investigation now into Aldo Anselmo's drug operations.

Robert Stewart and John McCallum were assigned a new secretary after their old one retired due to reasons of her pregnancy. The new replacement was expected for some time now. Robert overheard from the surveillance devices planted discreetly around Aldo Anselmo, that this secretary was a mole of his, used to infiltrate the police force, in order to extract personal information from both Robert and his police partner.

Aldo Anselmo planned to use this secretary plant on his payroll to spy on the police - and give him access to all their top-secret information on all the police investigations into the mob's activities. In fact, to provide tell-tale microfilm facts of their secret files, revealing how close the police were getting to uncovering their mob operations in order to nail them, so that Aldo could use decoys and sidestep the efforts of his police attackers and come up with diversion tactics and newer schemes to cover his tracks – and foil the policemen and policewomen's efforts against him.

Robert intercepted secret phone call conversations between the secretary and Aldo. Aldo spoke from his limousine private phone and she had the audacity to call her mob boss from the police department secretarial phone, inside police headquarters.

She insisted, "I want you to pay me big bucks for spying on Robert Stewart - and your plans to undermine his investigations against you as well as discredit him personally, when I plant large sums of money inside his office for you, and a bank deposit receipt to make it look like he is on the take and accepting bribes from New York City criminal figures. I am broke. I want you to pay me bigtime or else I am sure a lot of people will be interested in all your illegal plans against him!"

And that proved to be the biggest mistake of her life, next to being on the take for the mob, also threatening them at the same time. Aldo Anselmo blew up into volcanic pieces much like a great explosion over the phone to her: "You stupid woman. Do you have any idea who you are talking to? Don't you realise that I can make you disappear dead into the ground before you cry wolf. Don't you ever threaten me ever again, or else it will be the last thing you ever do. I promise you that!"

The naively stupid young police secretary almost sobbed in tears at her secretarial desk outside Robert's office and cried, "Ok. Ok. I'm sorry. But I expect to be paid. I cannot risk my life for nothing!"

Aldo Anselmo was still fuming as he blasted her over the phone in an extremely purplish irate manner: "You stupid twit. Who said I was not going to pay you? When you go to your house tonight after work, you will find a large envelope inside your mailbox, stuffed with inches-thick rolls of hundred dollar bills I had my courier deliver to you. So, stop complaining, stop talking like a little bitch, and do your job properly and get me all the information Robert has against me. And work to discredit him, so I can have him suspended from his duties and kicked out of the police force completely - when I make him look the part of the criminal, he is accusing me of being – and to my face!"

The dim-witted secretary seemed relieved and much satisfied at the mentioning of her payments being forthcoming, and snapped obediently and readily, "Ok, ok, I will do everything you say!"

Aldo snapped before he hung up the phone harshly on her ignorant face: "Good. Very good!"

The new police secretary would never make it to her home tonight to collect her mob money waiting for her inside her mailbox. Robert arrested her on the spot and sent his police partner John to retrieve and confiscate the money sent to her house inside her mailbox.

Meanwhile, Robert Stewart and John McCallum intensified their investigations against the Anselmo family illegal drug dealing operations.

Both Robert and John studied a current police map sketch drawing outlay they had designed of all the boats across the state's harbour. (Including aerial maps and police aerial photographs taken daily of the complete area, searching for clues and patterns of illegal conduct.) And one boat stationed there at all times in particular stood out like a sinner in church; the boat reeked suspect. It was a boat that remained idle with no legitimate reason for its local existence.

Meaning, it was not there for any legitimate purpose. Its purpose was for illegal reasons. And it was registered under the ownership of a phoney name.

Robert and John immediately suspected that drug shipments were coming from the Great Voyager, the name of the drug smuggling boat secretly owned by Mob Boss, Aldo Anselmo.

The police kept it under close surveillance with its operators until Robert and John's suspicions were proven accurate. The drug 'heroin' concealed inside fresh watermelons and hollow cabbages, was finally intercepted inside the speed boat, delivered by the supplier couriers' interstate and abroad. The boat made numerous trips back-and-forth, dropping off the drugs to discreetly-tailed Anselmo family truck driver couriers, waiting at the Brooklyn waterfront dock at midnight. Once the boat's many shipments were unloaded, the police followed the delivery trucks to various warehouses across the state - and then made their final arrests of all drug operators connected to the illegal narcotics trade. The police seized over $400 million worth of heroin, cash and illegal guns and arrested 128 drug operators in New York alone.

The arrests of interstate and those abroad traffickers from Italy, involved in the import-export trade of illegal drugs to New

York City, was also a successful undertaking. All international drug plants in relation to the case were also raided and seized by national and international police, all in cooperation together for the major busts.

Robert Stewart intercepted another Syndicate meeting Aldo Anselmo hosted with the local Mafia Chieftains inside his Brooklyn mansion. The topic of discussion was dealing with the police pressure cast on all of them. They felt flushed, not only by all the police raids and monetary losses incurred against them so far, but also, they all felt much leaped in severe chaos by all the heat the police were throwing their way, particularly by one cop in question: Robert Stewart.

So, they planned to remedy that grim situation and bleak outlook by declaring war on the police. They conspired to plant numerous bombs around the localities connected to Robert Stewart across the borough of Brooklyn, in an attempt to take all the cops out threatening their lives with Robert Stewart.

Aldo Anselmo was greatly worried about Robert Stewart's attacks against him. He even feared that Robert and the government may have him deported back to Italy if they uncovered evidence of his illegal dealings in the

United States. He was not yet naturalized as an official U.S. Citizen.

Aldo Anselmo recently sent his son back to Italy safely away from New York and the United States, until the Robert Stewart problem was dealt with.

The crime lord patriarch was fuming in anger against the menacing police commander. He thought vivid thoughts to himself as he wanted to inflict a great revenge against the cop in question. You should have stayed away from me and my family and empire, you bastard police commander! Robert Stewart is going to suffer a slow and painful death for trying to attack me.

Yes.

Robert Stewart gets in the way of progress. He destroys our businesses. He blocks the lifeblood of monetary flow for us bosses. That bastard son of a bitch cop is out of control. He must be stopped permanently.

Robert Stewart is going to die!

You are a fucking dead man, Robert Stewart! You hear me? You are a fucking dead man, you destructive, irrational and insane cop!

Yes, Robert Stewart. I have already constructed the detailed death plans for my particularly gory murder plot against you.

It will be a spectacular event of fireworks to be unleashed in the city – and witnessed by everyone in this State!

Your demise will be a fantastic and glorious sight for my eyes, Robert Stewart!

And after what I have in store for you, you will not be able to pull off any Houdini trick to extricate yourself out of that.

Certainly, and surely: your attacks against Aldo Anselmo will be where your life ends for good, police commander!

With the gory death I have waiting for you, this time you will become hopelessly trapped – never to return to pick fights against any of us ever again!

Robert Stewart – you should have stayed away from my family. Because of your insane foolishness, you will have to die along with all the others I plan to kill, in the firm desire to mark the infinite glory of my reign as ultimate boss of this country!

You cannot walk around destroying our empires and attacking us bosses like there is no tomorrow, without paying the ultimate price!

Your reign of terror against us will not continue – because you will become a dead man, long before you make another arrest of anyone in my world ever again!

Coming up against me is a very dangerous game – one that will end in disaster for you, crazy cop!

You call yourself vengeance. I call myself revenge!

But even though right now you have angered me to wanting to inflict great harm against you – I simply view my actions, my necessary actions, as a course of self-defence!

You will not experience any good things from warring with Aldo Anselmo!

I will attack you! I will trap you! I will torment you! And then I will finally end your chaotic life – forever!

And your death will make front-page headlines across the entire country. And I will certainly boast and celebrate the day of your glorious demise!

And you will never re-emerge alive as a threat to continue to be a nuisance to our world ever again!

Your fate is sealed, Robert Stewart!

Your death will become one of the greatest milestones for me!

And just like you, I am also a man who always keeps his promises! Especially when it comes to claiming my targets on the chair of death.

You will die Robert Stewart in front of the entire city and country!

And I will execute all others around you – especially your pesty police colleagues!

This is exciting for me: – in only a few moments, Robert Stewart will be dead!

And in the aftermath, I will make a donation to charity for ten million dollars – in order to keep my hands clean from suspicion by everyone, as having given the firm order behind Robert Stewart's death!

I must look totally innocent! No one can ever point fingers and blame me for his murder! And there will be no reprisals.

It will be a perfect murder. I will kill Robert Stewart in such a magnificent, ingenious and diabolical fashion, by avoiding detection by everyone at the same time!

So, be prepared, silly 'copper' – you're as good as dead!

Aldo Anselmo primarily vowed to kill Robert Stewart!

And the rest of the state's local bosses in order to preserve their interests, schemed together to assist Aldo Anselmo in accomplishing that one gigantic task: Robert Stewart's murder.

The Mob Bosses all agreed to plant a bomb inside Robert Stewart's personal home, his car and the 25th division precinct station house of Brooklyn, New York, the domain of his professional police work. They planned to kill Robert Stewart, his entire family and an army of cops working with him, whom in turn planned to bring down all the local mob biggies in New York State.

NOW, the syndicate leaders' united scheme to kill all their targets was set for tomorrow evening.

The syndicate leaders would employ the captains, who would lead the assassin soldiers to plant the numerous explosive devices in all the targeted areas, killing all their intended police victims with their families!

Aldo Anselmo ordered to his mob boss associates: "We will take them all down like dominoes. It is either them or us. Of course, we must be preserved for the future generations of our families and our kingdoms. So, the police must die. Their families must die. And the biggest threat to our existences, that menacing bastard cop Robert Stewart must be killed immediately! So, let us plant the bombs in all the targeted areas - and by tomorrow, we will have freedom to make our profits, once all those pesty police enemies of ours are removed from circulation and thrown into their graves where they belong!"

It was agreed unanimously by all the Mafia Crime Lords. And the plans to put in place the mass executions of their targets would proceed immediately, and their duties on that score would be fulfilled within twenty-four hours.

Robert Stewart stormed the Anselmo mansion with an army of heavily armed cops behind him. First, upon entering the estate, an Anselmo Mob Family hitman posted inside the front door hallway before the main living room, tried to block Robert's entrance inside the house, even ignoring the arrest warrant the police commander held in his right hand, with his boss's name Aldo Anselmo written on it.

The hitman threw a punch at Robert's face. Robert ducked the blow. But the second punch hit him in the stomach. Robert felt a tad winded, but that intrusion by this foolish attacker began the prelude to a deadly scuffle between them.

Robert side-kicked the hood into his knee and then just hammered his fists into his face, punching at an alarming rate.

The burly-looking hitman soldier bodyguard stumbled backwards slightly. But as he steadied himself expertly balanced onto his feet, he grabbed for his gun inside the holster underneath his grey-coloured suit jacket, which proved the last thing he would ever do. Robert quickly removed the gun from his own holster beneath his black leather jacket - and the first between them who drew their gun and fired became the survivor. Robert, holding the gun in his hand, first struck the hood's elbows with both hands to force a lagging and deliberate slowdown movement of his opponent's aim - and making him stumble unbalanced again for a moment, giving Robert enough time to quickly raise his weapon, steady his aim, and fire at the hitman's chest area, a fatal blow into his heart, killing the Anselmo thug instantly.

Quickly Robert Stewart and his great number of armed police reinforcements raced inside the living room area, where all the implicated mob bosses in the city were stationed inside, conspiring to wreak havoc and mass deaths across New York City.

The police were armed with warrants for the arrests of all of the five local mob syndicate leaders.

Four of them refused prison. It was as if they rehearsed their movements in premeditated gestures before this day. They planned to murder each other if the police ever warded too close to home.

Four of the Mafia bigshots removed hidden guns from their attired formal suits - and aimed it to the heads of the other Mafia Leader standing one metre opposite them. And they quickly fired a bullet at each other's heads. Four of the five main criminal players in New York City went down that day dead as the proverbial doornail.

Only one remained. A very shocked and surprised Aldo Anselmo, who was not apprised of the secret plan amongst the others to kill each other, if need be, to avoid police prosecution.

Only Aldo Anselmo remained alive out of all of them. He was armed with an otherwise untraceable gun, but he was surrounded by a swarm of armed cops. So, he did not remove his weapon from its holster in a bid to fight it out recklessly; he did not desire to achieve the similar outcome as his dead associates had by committing suicide.

Aldo Anselmo was instead arrested for his murderous mob crimes and officially booked downtown at police headquarters. The police had the goods on him. Real solid evidence. He would not be allowed back onto the streets ever again. He would rot in prison for the rest of his life, until his untimely death.

Aldo Anselmo insisted that death would not strike him, as he lay inside his local jail facility, pending his ordered trial, on sufficient evidence to counter his not guilty plea.

Aldo Anselmo vowed to fight the courts and be released from prison, to live out his great desire for revenge against Robert Stewart. But the judge he was assigned for his trial, was an unmerciful judge, who had little tolerance for gangsters such as Aldo Anselmo, and gangsters of the like, who flaunted their wealth - and showed off their sick desires to kill innocent people and boast of it in its aftermath.

The Judge would not tolerate such callous and unconscionable behaviour.

So, the judge sentenced the guilty Aldo Anselmo to life imprisonment, in the maximum-security prison facility in the state of New York, without possibility for parole!